DEMON CURSE MAGICK

Corwin Hargrove

Disclaimer: The ideas in this book are religious and spiritual in nature, and no harm is intended or implied beyond the realms of the fantastic. Readers are strongly encouraged to work within the confines of their own morality.

The content of the book is based on personal experience and conjecture and should be regarded as speculative entertainment and not professional, medical, or personal advice. The speculations within should not be perceived as professional, medical, relationship or lifestyle advice of any nature. The author does not recommend the use of these methods in place of conventional negotiations and mediation, and no claims about effects are implied.

The spiritual concepts and practices presented here are to be used at your own risk. The author is not responsible for the experiences you obtain from working with the methods presented. It is hereby stated clearly and in full that the author neither suggests nor condones that you ever act in a way that can cause harm and this book is provided with the understanding that the materials be used in accordance with the laws of your country or any country in which you are present.

Contents

Your Right to Revenge

The world is full of people who need to be punished, idiots who've wronged you, and cruel family members who enjoy seeing you suffer. Friends are jealous, and colleagues are backstabbers. And there's always somebody ready to take advantage. Deny this, and they *will* take advantage of your stupidity. You can fight back with demon magick.

Without sigils or supplies, you can curse somebody within a few minutes. This is more effective than any other approach I've used and guaranteed to be safe.

What you get here is a recipe book for disaster and disruption, hurling curses at those you loathe for the sake of peace, revenge, or the pure pleasure of punishing the guilty.

All you need is a sense of outrage, anger, injustice, or something like that. If your feelings are strong, they will excite the demons into a frenzy, and *their* violence will be directed toward your chosen victim.

In the everyday world, physical attacks and violence are abhorrent, and nobody has the right to attack. I created this book so that victims of violence have a way to fight back. When it comes to magick, you can seek justice without breaking the law, risking your safety, or being detected.

We're going to get straight into the magick. My last book was short, and some readers complained because they would prefer a lot of theory. Most didn't mind because if you want a grimoire for getting results, you don't need a book of pretentious theories and opinions.

In this book, you get the instructions you need and examples to show the way. These examples aren't 'case histories' but things I made up to act as inspiration and to guide you. It's a way of going a bit deeper than labelling a curse with a couple of words and should make it easier to make your choice. Use the magick, and you'll know why there's no need for more theory.

If you want to know what I think about magick and how it works, it's breadcrumbed through the book and my other books. But you find what magick can do and how it feels by using the rituals. If you want to experience its power, you must revel in its power.

Curse somebody and enjoy your revenge. You will learn all you need to know about cursing by cursing.

Demon curses can't and won't be stopped or reversed. What you set in motion will take place in some form, so make sure you want what you ask for.

What if the victim has put magickal protection of some kind in place? While far more *unlikely* than you think, it does happen. It may slow the results, but if you persist, you'll find you can trust this magick.

What about your own protection against such curses? The best advice is to piss people off in secret. Keep a low profile and manage your enemies well. Bring them down before they can harm you. That's genuinely all you need to know, and it never needs to be more complicated.

In *Goetia Pathworking*, I showed that the spirits are willing allies in your quest for transformation. The power has been refined in this book, using old methods to create simple, modern curses.

8

Why isn't pathworking used to contact the demons? In *Goetia Pathworking,* I showed my preferred way of working with the demons of Goetia. It's my most popular book, and I think rightfully so because the pathworking method is solid. If you want to work with the demons safely and effectively, readers have shown me it's a system that can work for anyone. But there are other ways to work with demons, and that's what you're discovering now.

Many of my other books contain various ways to harm people. But if you're after quick, effective curses, this book is what you're looking for. It's a different method, giving you a fast way to get your revenge. This is now the primary form of attack magick that I use. It's not often that I need it, and it shouldn't be for you. Every now and then, I come across some weak-minded fool who's lobbing curses at everyone they know. This kind of victim mentality is something to watch out for. If cursing is anything but an occasional practice, you should take a long look at yourself.

Instead of pathworking, this book uses Words of Power to invoke three demons in sequence, who each amplify and extend the powers of the others. It's not harmony or cooperation so much as a shared goal.

You tempt the demons by offering them a perfect victim, and they are unable to resist. This is a little-known key to getting demonic fever to fuel your rituals. You make your victim seem so deserving of attack that the demons will be encouraged by your rage to enact remarkable harm.

The Secrets of Demon Curse Magick

Why are there no sigils?
They aren't needed. It keeps this book much shorter than most. That makes it low-cost for you and wastes no ink or time.

Do you need any experience or special skills?
When using Words of Power, you need to get the pronunciation approximately right, and I know that this will annoy some people. Saying words out loud seems difficult. It isn't, and if you learn to say these words, you get real curses that work. Please note, and *never* forget, that I said 'approximately' right. I know countless panicked fools will shy away from this work, feeling that they must sound out perfect pronunciations. That is false. You only need to get them *approximately* right. Follow the instructions, and it will not go wrong.

How hard is it to learn the pronunciation?
Not hard at all because I hired an expert. For about fifty years, occultists have been turning Greek, Hebrew and other magickal words into phonetic approximations such as VAH-SAH-GOH or ELL-YOU-BAT-ELL for various demons, gods, angels and elemental forces. These phonetic approximations work if you take the time with them, and they've been the core of many practical books. But as I prepared this work, I realised that occult authors may be arrogant to assume

everybody can and will find it easy to follow these methods. My linguist-for-hire was tasked with making it all much easier for you. She created the pronunciations in this book, and I am satisfied with the result. She came at this with no prior knowledge of the occult, and the intention was to make the book so easy to use that a first-timer could pick it up, use it, and get results.

There is significant variation among English dialects, so the words have been chosen for consistency. Everything you need to succeed is included in the pronunciation guide.

What if English isn't your first language?
If you can read this, you can probably get by.

How long does it take to learn the pronunciations?
It takes a few minutes for each ritual. If you aren't prepared to spend a few minutes learning the codes for contacting the demons, then you probably don't want to perform the magick strongly enough. You should have more than a casual desire to cause harm.

How long does the effect last?
This question usually means you want to curse somebody once and have it work on them forever. There are ways to make curses last forever, but they are not obvious. Magickal effects never last long if you're honest with yourself and study magick closely. Magick causes change, and then it stops making a difference, and it's up to you to build on the results that magick gave you. When you use curses to cause accidents and injuries, those effects can cause harm and discomfort for

years, even when the magickal moment of the accident is extremely brief. You do not curse somebody for a week, month or year. You curse them with an appropriate and cleverly chosen curse, and the effects will last for the right amount of time.

How can cursing be safe when curses bounce back three times stronger?

They never do, so give up on that old superstition! The magick is safe, and if you're too afraid to use it, it's probably because you're worried that the demons will turn on you, that the ritual will backfire, and that there will be karma or payback. If you believe in karma, you should study reincarnation instead of magick.

Should you trust my claim that the magick is safe?

If you don't believe me, you are free to banish, cast circles, and do whatever you want before and after the ritual. None of it will make a difference. Instead, follow the instructions and the format I've set out for you. That makes it safe. How can it be safe if no restraining words or holy words shackle the demons into obedience? The words of power are a form of instruction that guides the demon to take on a predetermined role.

What do the Words of Power mean?

They will sound like nothing of any meaning to you, or you may pick up traces of words if you know the languages of magick. It means nothing, even when you sense meaning in the words. Treat these words of power only as sounds that unlock the assigned powers of the demon in the safest way for you.

How fast does it work?

When you take a painkiller, the effects might be felt within twenty minutes. For some medications, it's more like two hours, but it's still predictable. You've probably found that it's not the same with magick. The timing is rarely predictable. With curses, the timing is not predictable. The demons seek out a way to harm where they can, but they will not sacrifice the quality of the result for speed. You should expect results but don't panic if you see nothing for some time. I usually expect something to happen within three days, but you may also find something lingering from the ritual gets to your victim a month later. If there's a perfect time to act, the demons will know when that moment is coming, and they will wait for it. Consider this when judging the effectiveness of a ritual.

If it doesn't work, how long should you wait before doing the ritual again?

You should not decide that a ritual has failed without evidence, and that it is why these curses have all been crafted with the goal of creating noticeable harm. If you get a result, you won't be left guessing or wondering if your victim was harmed. You'll see them suffer. The only exceptions are those where there's no way you could see those results. Like when you curse somebody you have not seen for years. Remember that pervert who assaulted you fifteen years ago and got away with it? Even if you've never seen that bastard since you can curse them now for the sheer pleasure of revenge. While you probably won't get the full effect of seeing them suffer, you will sense a degree of satisfaction.

Can I tune it to be less destructive so kids don't get hurt and nobody feels suicidal?

There is no way to predict how anyone will respond to being cursed, so there are no guarantees of success, and there are no safeguards you can put in to protect the victims. Demons are rarely going to drive somebody to suicide. Ordinary life is already far too good enough at that, sadly. But know that if you cause harm, you *are* causing harm. Use one of the less aggressive rituals if that's uncomfortable for you. Even then, be willing to live with whatever you choose.

Do I need to know the real name of my target?
It's ideal if you do, but it's not the only way. If someone hurts you anonymously, you can still get revenge. Imagine if a relative of yours were harmed in some way or killed by the malice or idiocy of another person. You may never find out who was to blame, but you can curse them easily as you know who they are to you. The ritual involves thinking about the person and what they've done, so it easily works on people you don't know directly.

Can I curse movie stars and politicians?
You can, but it won't work unless the person has directly affected you. See the question above. If somebody has destroyed your life by murdering a family member, you can harm them even without knowing them, as they have impacted you so greatly. But people you blame at a distance – such as politicians - don't have sufficient connection to your timeline to be affected.

Can I combine several rituals at once to really hurt somebody?

No, not all on the same day. This isn't a book of magick tricks, so treat it more like a grimoire of knowledge than a plaything. Use one ritual with intent, and if you get impatient, use another. If you're doing more than that, it's a bit like pissing into the wind. Don't waste your time. It's too precious.

What if I want to curse everyone in the office? Or an entire company?

This magick is designed to work against individuals. If you have time, you can target everyone, but your rage is better directed at one or two people. For each person, perform a complete ritual just for them. You can't do a ritual and put three people in there, hoping it will affect them all. The focus on a chosen victim is important, so don't try to do too much.

Is this difficult to learn?

The ritual is simple and does not need to be any more elaborate. You should, however, follow the instructions and attempt to follow them with respect for the steps that have been developed for this ritual. Before that, choose your victim. You'll find how in the next chapter.

Can I practice the pronunciation beforehand, or is it dangerous to say the words?

You can and should practice. The words do nothing when they are spoken. They are activated when you bring your desire into play alongside the ritual format. Until then, they are only sounds.

I can't find time to be alone, so can I say the words silently in my head?
No. Find a time to be alone. It's not that difficult.

Choosing Your Victim

When it comes to the art of demonic curse magick, selecting the right victim is paramount. The demons you summon are eager to execute your will, but their effectiveness hinges on the clarity of your intent and the suitability of your target.

If you choose wisely, these infernal beings will be unable to resist the lure of your request, bringing about the desired chaos with precision and fervour. The demons are powerful, and their power is magnified when directed at a deserving target. This isn't about indiscriminate vengeance; it's about strategic disruption. And when I say 'deserving', I only mean that they deserve punishment in *your* eyes. If you feel it and believe it, then let justice be done.

Why the Right Victim Matters

Demons thrive on a degree of specificity. When you provide them with a well-defined target and a selected outcome, their energy is concentrated and potent. A vague or ill-chosen victim dilutes this power, leading to suboptimal results.

The right victim is one who truly embodies the qualities or actions you seek to punish or disrupt. They must have wronged you in a way that justifies the severity of your magick. This alignment of purpose and target is what makes your curse irresistible to the demon.

The Demons are Itching to Work for You

Understand that the demons you call upon are not passive entities. They are active, dynamic forces with a strong urge to manifest their powers. They seek to demonstrate their prowess, and nothing excites them more than a clearly defined mission. When you summon a demon like Belial to disrupt someone's wealth or Dantalion to twist their thoughts, you are tapping into an ancient reservoir of dark energy that yearns for expression.

Clear Desire

Be explicit in your intent and your desire. If your aim is psychological terror, that is your desire. Feel it. Know it and want it. This desire is all that matters. You do not need to worry about how, when and why the curse will work, and you should not focus on the details. You can fantasise and imagine various results, but you should also know that your desire to cause harm should not be too narrow. If, for example, you want somebody to move out of your house, that's all you want. It's tempting to come up with a plan, working out every detail that could force them to leave. But that is not the best way to do magick. Focus on your desire and not how it will happen.

By choosing the right victim and the appropriate demon, you ensure that your curse will be executed with maximum potency. You direct the magick at somebody who really needs to be punished in your eyes. And you choose the right demon who will deliver the style of punishment you desire.

The Ritual

Performing the ritual is extremely simple. The Words of Power access the demons in a specific way, and that means there's not much for you to do. If you prefer using incense and candles, with chants and incantations, you can do all that. None of it matters. These are the steps you follow:

Identify Your Victim: Choose someone whose actions or qualities warrant the disruption or harm you seek.

Define Your Intent: Be clear in your mind about what you want to achieve. If you want somebody to be badly injured, that's what you want. You don't need to specify that they get their legs broken. Just know that you want them to be hurt.

I could explain this for chapter after chapter, as some authors do, but that's the only example you need. Read it until you understand. If you genuinely want to curse somebody, it will take almost no effort to sense what sort of a result you would like. If you're not certain, look through the book and see if a particular curse appeals.

Select the Appropriate Curse: The curses are quite varied. Choose one that aligns with your goal. The examples I've given, while possibly a little corny on the surface, show you how and when each curse would work best for you. Don't spend too much time on this because anything will work, and it's better to get started than to wait for everything to be perfectly prepared.

Practice Pronunciation: It's been made clear that you don't need to get the pronunciation perfectly right. You should, however, learn the words so you can say them easily. That's all. You're not trying to impress anybody with your pronunciation. You are learning sounds that call to demons. Once you feel comfortable, you're ready for the next part, which you can perform at any time.

Summon with Words: Use the Words of Power and ritual instructions provided in this book to call upon the demon. That's what starts in the next paragraph.

The instructions that follow are based on the same concepts as found in previous books, so if they sound familiar, that means I'm not wasting your time. I will never add unnecessary complications to make it look better. You get the instructions that work.

You can perform curse rituals at any time of the day or night, on any day of the week, and at any time of year. Some people find that working at night makes them nervous. This can be okay as long as it doesn't get out of hand with your fear taking over. If you find it too frightening, work in the day. You may hear a few bumps and creaks, but this is either a coincidence or a small sign that the magick is working.

More important than timing is demarcating the ritual from your ordinary life, and this is why you create a magickal state of mind. Prepare well by reading all the instructions and choosing carefully.

Settle down, away from people, things, devices, and interruptions. The state of mind you need is about intention and focus. It brings you to the ritual. When you are present, you pass on all that you desire to the demons, and that makes it work more effectively.

I advise you to take the time to settle into the ritual, to let your ordinary world fall away, and to spend some time feeling and experiencing the ritual as a time of magick.

What I recommend for almost all magick is to take an hour to settle down first. With this magick, you need less time. I'd say for most people, ten minutes is enough. You should always treat this as your sacred time, though. You don't 'pass the time' to get it over with or to rush through to the ritual. Settling *is* a part of the ritual, so dampen the noise, switch off devices, be alone, be quiet, and shut up and shut down.

If you want to, give it an hour but know that ten minutes will be enough. There's no need to pretend that working harder will make it better. All you're doing is cutting off from some aspects of reality while still being able to feel your enraged emotions.

You can think about whatever you like, but it's best if you think about things that make you calm during this phase. You'll get to the magick soon enough, so you can let that inner rage stay out of your mind without effort. If you prefer to go for a walk, that works too and can occupy you easily. You can walk without any purpose other than to set time aside for magick.

And that is why, during the time you set aside, whether it's five minutes or an hour, you don't work on the ritual. If you find yourself thinking about the ritual, do not chide yourself or give up. Move on from those thoughts and think about something else. Don't stress about this, or you amplify your stress. Relax and know that you are setting aside time for the ritual, and that is all that matters.

In some rituals, I suggest preparing a reward for yourself, but I do not suggest that with these curses. If you've read about that in other books, ignore it for now.

The ritual itself is short and simple. Trust that I only give you what you need, and I do not believe it helps to dress up the ritual with unnecessary theatrics. You will need to speak the words out loud, but there is no need to act or perform them in any specific way.

You may feel that your voice changes as you go through the ritual. Do not be alarmed or frightened if this happens. You are still in control.

You can sit or stand, but I have found that after initially settling, it helps to stand up for the ritual itself. It's like giving yourself a signal that the real moment has arrived.

You can face any direction but don't have anything too interesting in your field of view.

The ritual itself consists of you thinking about your victim, feeling the emotions that are produced and then speaking the words of power. That's all there is to it, and it's even easier in practice than it sounds on paper.

You do not need to do anything else. When you say the final word, you have completed the curse and simultaneously closed the ritual.

What I've described there is enough for the ritual to work, but let me give you one example to make sure it's all set out clearly.

Imagine you were conned by a trusted friend. We'll call him Dave in this example. Dave pretended to be a friend but only ever wanted your money. He also enjoyed belittling you. The time has come to set things straight. In this example, which curse shall we use?

Well, first things first. Remember, before choosing the curse, you should define your intent. What do you want to happen to Dave?

You might go over the possibilities until you end up knowing that you want Dave to suffer more than he made you suffer. You want him to feel so insane that he begins to feel guilty for everything he's done wrong.

Now, you choose the appropriate curse. In this example, you might choose to give Dave a serving of Psychic Turbulence. You can see what the demons can do. You know how you feel about what Dave did to you. Everything is in place.

Now, spend ten minutes or so settling into the mood for the ritual, and then you *decide* to begin. As I said earlier, standing up can help to symbolise this opening, but you don't have to stand. Simply deciding is enough, and no ceremony is required.

You now think about Dave and the whole story of what he did to you. This might take as little as three or four seconds or several minutes. Your intention is to *feel* the anger, rage, or sense of injustice that naturally stirs within you when you think of everything Dave has done to you. If the words I've used there don't fit, that's okay. You will know what you feel.

If you find yourself thinking your emotions aren't strong enough, examine whether you really want to curse or not. I will not curse somebody unless the very thought of their actions makes me angry. It doesn't take much to get me there. But don't think you need to be seething with rage. Demons are so hungry for these emotions that they will feel the merest of emotions and will thrive on their energy. (Nothing is taken from you, and the demons are not literally fed. It's more like dangling a carrot.)

As soon as you feel something about Dave, you look down at the book and speak the Words of Power. Those emotions may stay, change, or go away altogether, but your focus should be on the words of power.

Repeat the words three times. In this case, you would say these words:

Mar-bas Ha-da-at Ha-so-rer-et For-ne-us A-vur Gal Pni-mi Shel Ge-shem Ga-ap A-vur Ri-fyon

Mar-bas Ha-da-at Ha-so-rer-et For-ne-us A-vur Gal Pni-mi Shel Ge-shem Ga-ap A-vur Ri-fyon

Mar-bas Ha-da-at Ha-so-rer-et For-ne-us A-vur Gal Pni-mi Shel Ge-shem Ga-ap A-vur Ri-fyon

When that is done, you may feel some lingering emotion. If so, let it be there until it goes away. When you say the final word for the third time, the ritual is over. You know this, and the demons know this. You don't need to show it in any other way.

You can now put the book away and get back to your ordinary life. Find something to occupy your body or mind that is pleasant but not magickal. Focus on the ordinary sensations of existence, such as eating, drinking, walking, talking, or anything non-magickal.

If you feel that there's a lingering presence, try not to fight that feeling. The demons cannot harm you, given the way that they were called, but they may remain close as they work on the best way to make your result become real.

Read the whole book at least once before you begin your first ritual to ensure you know exactly what your choices are.

Decide who you are going to curse.

Form your desire into an intention.

Choose an appropriate ritual.

Learn the pronunciation required for your ritual and become familiar with the sound of the words without obsessing over precision.

At any time, when you are ready, prepare for your ritual by settling as described.

Think about your victim, and without trying to justify anything, notice the feelings that rage within you. When you think about your victim, this rage will rise.

Read the words of power from beginning to end. Do this three times. You do not need to hold on to feelings.

When you speak the final word for the third time, the ritual is over. It is safe to assume that the demons have been dismissed by the structure of the ritual.

Get back to normal.

Each ritual needs to be performed only once to get the result you desire.

Let a few days pass before you perform your next curse ritual (whether against the same person or not) unless there is an extreme need.

Twenty-Five Demon Curse Rituals

All twenty-five rituals are set out on the following pages, with the main information coming first, followed by a pronunciation guide. At the end, the words of power appear clearly, and you can read them from the page. If you prefer to write them down so you can close the book, then go ahead.

You should, of course, have read the instructions for the ritual itself. After the ritual is over, don't wait for signs of a result. If you stop waiting and wanting, you will see results. Some rituals include directions concerning time, with the results meant to come more swiftly or to last for a longer period. Take this into account, but continue to avoid lusting after an immediate result. The results may be immediate, but I hope you will have the patience to let the magick work.

Pronunciation guides are provided throughout, but here are some general guidelines to consider.

G or g is always hard, like in 'go'.

Tz or tz is the sound found in the middle of words like 'cats', 'Betsy' or 'pizza'.

Uh is like the sound found in the insulting exclamation 'duh'.

That's enough information for you to begin.

Memory Erosion

Memory Erosion is one of those rituals that gets right under the skin, slowly causing someone to lose their grip on reality. Think of it like a slow leak in a tyre – it doesn't blow out all at once but gradually deflates until you're left stranded. This ritual is designed to make someone forget the things that matter most to them, from important facts to cherished memories and even their own sense of self. It's not flashy, but it's effective.

I think we can all picture the stereotypical executive in his prime, always stepping on others to climb the corporate ladder. He's sharp, ruthless, and never misses a beat. But then, you curse him, and little by little, he starts forgetting key details during meetings. First, it's minor things – the names of clients and the specifics of a project. His colleagues notice but don't say much. As the weeks go by, though, it gets worse. He forgets entire strategies, crucial deadlines, and even important appointments. His reputation takes a hit, and before long, he's demoted and sidelined, and all that ambition counts for nothing. That's the power of Memory Erosion.

Or take a neighbourhood gossip who thrives on spreading rumours and stirring up trouble. She's the type who always has a new piece of scandalous news, delighting in the chaos she creates. But after a few months of this ritual working its magick, she starts to forget her own stories. She contradicts herself, mixes up details, and loses track of who she's slandered. Her credibility crumbles and people start to see her for what she really is – unreliable and confused. The community breathes a sigh of relief as her influence wanes.

The beauty of Memory Erosion is in its simplicity and inevitability. The effects start small but grow more significant over time. It's a slow burn but one that's incredibly hard to reverse.

Demons to Invoke

Vassago: Known for the ability to discover the truth and know the past, Vassago can manipulate these powers to cause the target to lose their grip on their past and forget crucial details.

Buer: Specialises in mental and emotional healing but can also bring about a weak state of mind that leads to forgetfulness. Buer can subtly erode the target's memory, making them forget important facts and personal details.

Foras: Known for concealing valuable items, Foras can extend this power to hide memories and important information from the target's mind, causing gradual memory loss.

Words of Power for Memory Erosion

Vah-sah-goh Beh-tohk Hah-or

Vah: *vah* as in "**va**ledictory"
sah: *sah* as in "**su**n"
goh: like "Go"
Beh: *beh* as in "**be**t"
tohk: like "Tock"
Hah: like laughing "ha!"
or: *aur* as in "**aur**a"

Boo-er Beh-ray-oh-no-teh-nu

Boo: like "Boo!"
er: like "air"
Beh: be as in "**be**t"
ray: like "Ray"
oh: like "awe"
no: like "gnaw"
teh: *te* as in "**te**pid"
nu: like "new" but rhymes with "shoo"

Foras She-ro-eh Yo-ter

For: like "four"
ras: *raz* rhymes with "jazz"
She: *sheh* as in "**she**d"
ro: like "raw"
eh: *eh* as in "**e**lf"
Yo: *yaw* as in "**yaw**n"
ter: like "tare"

Vah-sah-goh Beh-tohk Hah-or
Boo-er Beh-ray-oh-no-teh-nu
Foras She-ro-eh Yo-ter

Swift Memory Erosion

Swift Memory Erosion is for when you need results fast. It's like pulling the plug on someone's mental hard drive, causing a rapid decline in their memory. Unlike the slow leak in a tyre, this ritual works more like a sudden puncture, deflating the target's cognitive abilities almost overnight. It's brutal and efficient, perfect for situations where time is of the essence.

Imagine a competitive salesperson who always beats you to the punch, sealing deals before you even get a chance. One week, they're at the top of their game, and the next, they can't remember the terms of a contract or the names of key clients. Meetings become a minefield of forgotten details and embarrassing stumbles. Their once-impeccable reputation crumbles as quickly as a house of cards in a windstorm.

Or think of a colleague who's been a thorn in your side for years. With Swift Memory Erosion, their conversations become jumbled messes, filled with half-remembered promises and forgotten points. Meetings turn into disasters as they struggle to recall basic facts and figures. Even somebody who once seemed invincible is suddenly vulnerable and exposed.

This ritual's power lies in its speed. While traditional Memory Erosion is a slow burn, Swift Memory Erosion hits like a sledgehammer. The effects are immediate and undeniable, causing the target's memory to fail them when they need it most.

Demons to Invoke

Botis: Known for causing disfigurement and reading thoughts and feelings, Botis can swiftly disrupt the target's mental clarity, leading to immediate and noticeable memory loss.

Balam: Specialises in reducing attention and presence. Balam can create a rapid decline in the target's cognitive abilities, making them forget crucial information almost instantaneously.

Murmus: With the power to trap individuals in cycles of thought and cause indecision, Murmus can quickly erode the target's memory, causing immediate confusion and forgetfulness.

Words of Power for Swift Memory Erosion

Botis Ta-mid Be-or

Bo: *baw* as in "**baw**l"
tis: *tis* as in "no**tice**"
Ta: tah as in "U**tah**"
mid: like "mid"
Beh: *beh* as in "**bet**"
or: *aur* as in "**aur**a"

Balam She-mit-bo-nen Bi-fen-im

Ba: *bah* as in "ba**ba**"
lam: Like "lamb"
She: *sheh* as in "**she**d"
mit: like "meet"
bo: *baw* as in "**baw**l"
nen: *nen* as in "li**nen**" and rhymes with "ten"
Bi: like "bee"
Fen: *fen* as in "**fen**ce"
im: *eem* rhymes with "meme"

Murmus She-me-su-gal Lish-bor

Mur: *mur* as in "**mur**mur"
mus: *muss* as in "**mus**t"
She: *sheh* as in "**she**d"
me: *meh,* as in "**me**t"
su: like "sue"
gal: like "gull"
Lish: *lish* as in "de**lish**"
bor: like "bore"

Botis Ta-mid Be-or
Balam She-mit-bo-nen Bi-fen-im
Murmus She-me-su-gal Lish-bor

Eviction Hex

When you want somebody to move out or move away from you, this is the best ritual I have ever found. You can use this on unwelcome neighbours, lodgers, or relatives who live with you. It can even be used against strangers to get them to vacate a property you want to own. (Taking this even further, you can use this when buying a house to make the owners so keen to leave that they will accept a low offer on their property.)

Rituals of this nature often create a series of inconveniences and discomforts that drive a person away. While effective, it can be risky as these people are usually living close to you. This ritual is different and works with more subtlety, persuading your victim to think they have made a wise and independent decision. It's the finest form of influence magick. It won't always work as fast as you want, so be patient.

Don't be put off by neighbours or relatives who seem entrenched in their homes. Even the most stubborn people can be made to feel the effects of this curse.

Demons to Invoke

Foras: Specialises in causing decay and deterioration. Foras can introduce mould, mildew, and unpleasant odours, making the living environment intolerable.

Botis: Capable of causing confusion and disruptions. Botis can manipulate circumstances to cause frequent appliance breakdowns and other domestic inconveniences.

Agares: The demon specialises in causing hesitation and ruining stability. Agares can subtly influence the target to feel increasingly uneasy and uncomfortable in their home, pushing them to seek new living arrangements.

Words of Power for the Eviction Hex

Fo-ras Pa-chad Ha-ba-yit

For: like "four"
ras: *raz* rhymes with "jazz"
Pa: *pah* as in "Pa**pa**"
chad: starts with hard *h*/soft *k* sound and rhymes with "mud"
Hah: like laughing "ha!"
ba: *bah* as in "ba**ba**"
yit: like "yeet"

Bo-tis Ha-da-ba

Bo: *baw* as in "**baw**l"
tis: *tis* as in "no**tice**"
Hah: like laughing "ha!"
da: *dah* as in "**dah**l"
ba: *bah* as in "ba**ba**"

A-ga-res Ga-nav Ha-ta-a-nu-got

A: rhymes with singing "la!"
ga: *ga* as in "ga**ga**"
res: *rez* as in "**res**erve"
Ga: *ga* as in "ga**ga**"
nav: *nahv* as in "**nav**igable"
Hah: like laughing "ha!"
ta: tah as in "U**tah**"
a: rhymes with singing "la!"
nu: like "new" but rhymes with "shoo"
got: like "got"

Fo-ras Pa-chad Ha-ba-yit
Bo-tis Ha-da-ba
A-ga-res Ga-nav Ha-ta-a-nu-got

Sexual Disruption

Render your enemy sexually dysfunctional and prone to revealing their perversions publicly. This is a ruthless ritual designed to bring someone's most intimate and private life crashing down in ruins. You will summon significant disruptions that impact their sexual confidence and behaviour. It's like turning their sexual existence into a source of embarrassment and shame.

Sexual Disruption can be like planting a virus in their libido, causing it to malfunction in the most humiliating ways. Imagine the self-proclaimed Casanova of your social circle, always boasting about his conquests and making others uncomfortable with his advances. He's built his reputation on charm and seduction, but as the ritual takes effect, his sexual prowess starts to falter. He faces inexplicable dysfunction and becomes paranoid about his performance. Whispers of his embarrassing encounters spread, and soon, his confident façade crumbles. He's no longer the charming seducer but a figure of ridicule and pity.

It can work just as well against a 'perfect' suburban mom, who's always vocally judging others for their lifestyle choices. She's known for her moral high ground, but in private, she harbours some rather unconventional desires. As the ritual works, her secrets start slipping out. Her carefully crafted image shatters, leaving her to deal with the humiliation and fallout within her pristine community.

The beauty of Sexual Disruption lies in its dual attack. Not only does it impair the target's sexual functionality, leading to personal and intimate frustration, but it also drags their hidden perversions into the light, causing public humiliation. It's like a ticking time bomb set to explode at the most inconvenient moments, wreaking havoc on both personal and public fronts. The effects start subtly but become increasingly apparent and destructive over time.

Demons to Invoke

Sitri: Known for causing love and lust, Sitri can be asked to manipulate these feelings to create dysfunction and public embarrassment.

Zepar: Typically associated with influencing love and sexual attraction, Zepar can invert this power to cause sexual dysfunction and frustration.

Asmodai: As a demon of lust, Asmodai can twist desires into something uncontrollable and humiliating.

Words of Power for Sexual Disruption

Sitri She-me-kal-kel Ma-yim

Sit: like "seat"
ri: *ree* as in "**ree**d"
She: *sheh* as in "**she**d"
me: *meh* as in "**me**t"
kal: starts with *k* and rhymes with "gull"
kel: *kehl* as in "**kel**p"
Ma: *mah* as in "ma**ma**"
yim: *yeem* rhymes with "ream"

Zepar She-me-ya-besh Dva-rim

Ze: *zeh* as in "**ze**nith"
par: like "par"
She: *sheh* as in "**she**d"
me: *meh* as in "**me**t"
ya: *yah* as in "**yu**m"
besh: starts with *b* and rhymes with "mesh"
Dva: The first sound is *duh*, then *vah*, as in "**va**ledictory"
rim: like "ream"

Asmodai She-mash-pil

As: rhymes with "jazz"
mo: like "maw"
dai: like "dye"
She: *sheh* as in "**she**d"
mash: *mush* as in "**mush**room"
pil: like "peel"

Sitri She-me-kal-kel Ma-yim
Zepar She-me-ya-besh Dva-rim
Asmodai She-mash-pil

Disruptive Mind

Disruptive Mind is designed to invade and corrupt the thoughts of your target. It fills their mind with disturbing images and chaotic ideas, causing ongoing mental distress. It's a sustained assault on their mental stability, turning thoughts into a nightmare from which they cannot escape. It's a subtle form of torture.

Think about a respected teacher, once known for their calm and insightful lessons. As the ritual takes hold, their mind is plagued with intrusive and chaotic thoughts. Their lectures become confused; their explanations muddled. Students notice the change, and the respect they once commanded begins to wane. They become a shadow of their former self, overwhelmed by the turmoil within their mind.

Or what about a close friend who has always been your pillar of support but is now undermining you? As the Disruptive Mind ritual sets in, they struggle with disturbing thoughts that they can't escape. Conversations that were once coherent and reassuring become fragmented and unsettling. They withdraw from social interactions, unable to trust their own mind, and the shared bond begins to unravel. Every decision becomes a struggle against the chaos in their thoughts, and every interaction a challenge to maintain composure.

Demons to Invoke

Marchosias: Specialises in dissuading enemies and negotiating forcefully. Marchosias can corrupt the target's thoughts, filling their mind with unsettling images and ideas, leading to continuous mental distress.

Amon: With the power to create chaos in groups and stimulate romantic feelings, Amon can twist these abilities to fill the target's mind with chaotic and disturbing thoughts, causing them to lose mental stability.

Valefar: Specialises in stimulating disloyalty and breaking secrecy. Valefar can invade the target's mind, causing continuous intrusive and chaotic thoughts that disrupt their mental peace and stability.

Words of Power for Disruptive Mind

Mar-ko-si-as She-me-val-bel Ra-a-yon

March: like "mark" but ends with hard *h*/soft *k* sound
o: like "awe"
si: like "see"
as: rhymes with "jazz"
She: *sheh* as in "**she**d"
me: *meh* as in "**me**t"
val: *vahl* as in "**val**edictory"
bel: like "bell"
Ra: *rah* as in "**ra**men"
a: rhymes with singing "la!"
yon: like "yawn"

Amon Ha-be-ten Ha-ka-o-ti

A: rhymes with singing "la!"
mon: starts with *m* and rhymes with "yawn"
Ha: like laughing "ha!"
be: *beh* as in "**be**t"
ten: like "ten"
Ha: like laughing "ha!"
ka: *kah* as in "**cu**p"
o: like "awe"
ti: like "tea"

Va-le-far Le-ha-ros Ka-os

Vah: *vah* as in "**va**ledictory"
le: *leh* as in "**le**t"

far: like "far"
Le: *leh* as in "**let**"
ha: like laughing "ha!"
ros: *rawz* as in "**ros**in"
Ka: *kah* as in "**cup**"
os: *awz* as in "**Aus**sie"

Mar-ko-si-as She-me-val-bel Ra-a-yon
Amon Ha-be-ten Ha-ka-o-ti
Va-le-far Le-ha-ros Ka-os

Financial Ruin

Financial Ruin is a ruthless ritual that is set up to dismantle your target's financial stability. By channelling negative energy, you can lead them into a spiral of debt and chaos. It systematically destabilises their financial foundation, leaving them struggling to stay afloat.

Imagine someone who flaunts their wealth and mocks those less fortunate. As this ritual takes effect, their financial decisions start to backfire. Investments plummet, unexpected expenses pile up, and their once-solid income becomes precarious. They find themselves borrowing more and more, sinking deeper into debt. Their arrogance turns to desperation as they watch their financial empire crumble.

Or a business rival who has always seemed untouchable. Suddenly, their company faces one setback after another. Major clients pull out, contracts fall through, and lawsuits drain their resources. The confident entrepreneur quickly becomes a frantic and desperate figure, scrambling to salvage their failing business. The financial chaos disrupts not just their business but their personal life as well, as they struggle to cope with the mounting pressures.

The beauty of Financial Ruin is in its thoroughness. It's not a quick hit but a steady, relentless decline that leaves the target with little hope of recovery. It affects all aspects of their financial life, from income to investments, causing a cascade of failures that lead to complete ruin. As always, the examples are only a hint of how powerful this can be. Imagine how easily you can harm anyone by using this curse.

Demons to Invoke

Belial: Induces financial pressure and stress, manipulating money to create misfortune, accidents, and real and perceived stress.

Haures. The demon can put somebody into a looping maze of misfortune, causing weakness and suffering but also building the momentum of cyclic poverty.

Dantalion. This demon can assist with any concern and here applies wisdom to the efforts of the other demons, shaping the result.

Words of Power for Financial Ruin

Be-li-al Be-ye-su-rei Ha-o-vdan

Beh: *beh* as in "**bet**"
li: *lee* as in "**lea**n"
al: rhymes with "gull"
Beh: *beh* as in "**bet**"
ye: *yeh* as in "**yet**"
su: like "sue"
rei: like "Ray"
Hah: like laughing "ha!"
o: like "awe"
vdan: first sound is *vuh* then *dahn* as in "**dahn**aid"

Ha-ru-es She-me-na-petz

Hah: like laughing "ha!"
ru: *roo* as in "kanga**roo**"
es: *ess* as in "m**ess**"
She: *sheh* as in "**she**d"
me: *meh* as in "**me**t"
na: like "nah"
petz: Like "pet" but ends with the *tzuh* sound

Dan-ta-li-on She-mash-lim Et Ha-kol

Dan: *dahn* as in "**dan**aid"
ta: tah as in "U**tah**"
li: *lee* as in "**lea**n"
on: *awn* as in "y**awn**"
She: *sheh* as in "**she**d"

mash: *mush* as in "**mush**room"
lim: starts with *l* and rhymes with "ream"
Et: *eht* as in "**et**iquette"
Hah: like laughing "ha!"
kol: like "coal"

Be-li-al Be-ye-su-rei Ha-o-vdan
Ha-ru-es She-me-na-petz
Dan-ta-li-on She-mash-lim Et Ha-kol

Relationship Discord

Relationships can be the foundation of happiness and stability, but when you sow the seeds of discord, that foundation crumbles. The Relationship Discord ritual is designed to inject chaos into a romantic relationship, leading to mistrust, jealousy, and constant arguments. This isn't just a minor spat; it's a deep, festering wound that slowly but surely destroys any sense of harmony.

Imagine the couple that seems perfect on the outside. They're always together, sharing laughs and whispered secrets. But as this ritual starts to work, small doubts creep into their minds. She wonders why he's late home from work again. He notices her smile a bit too brightly at a friend's joke. These small seeds of doubt grow into accusations, jealousy, and constant fights. Their once-perfect relationship becomes a battleground of suspicion and hurt.

Then there's the newly engaged couple planning their future with joy. They're excited, hopeful, and full of dreams. But as the ritual takes hold, the harmony dissolves. He becomes suspicious of her every move, and she feels constantly judged and mistrusted. Every conversation turns into a confrontation, and every plan is a source of tension. The engagement becomes a nightmare, and their dreams of a future together disintegrate into ashes.

There is another curse, later in the book, that is more direct and harmful to a relationship.

Demons to Invoke

Leraye: Specialises in revealing enemies and causing conflict. Leraye can turn small doubts and misunderstandings into major sources of tension and discord within the relationship.

Zepar: Typically associated with influencing love and sexual attraction, Zepar can twist these powers to create jealousy and mistrust, making the partners question each other's fidelity and intentions.

Orobas: Known for attracting admiration and improving reputation, Orobas can be invoked to manipulate the perceptions of one partner, making them feel unappreciated and leading to feelings of resentment and jealousy.

Words of Power for Relationship Discord

Le-ra-ye She-me-o-rer Sa-fek

Le: *leh* as in "**le**t"
ra: *rah* as in "**ra**men"
ye: *yeh* as in "**ye**t"
She: *sheh* as in "**she**d"
me: *meh* as in "**me**t"
o: like "awe"
rer: like "rare"
Sa: *sah* as in "**su**n"
fek: *fehk* as in "**feck**less"

Zepar Shel Ha-sod Ve-ha-yi-rah

Ze: *zeh* as in "**ze**nith"
par: like "par"
Shel: like "shell"
Ha: like laughing "ha!"
sod: like "sawed"
Ve: *veh* as in "**ve**t"
ha: like laughing "ha!"
yi: *yee* as in "**yee**ha!"
rah: *rah* as in "**ra**men"

O-ro-bas Ha-si-na-ah Ha-nis-ta-ret

O: *Oh* as in "**o**men"
ro: like "raw"
bas: starts with *b* and rhymes with "jazz"
Ha: like laughing "ha!"

si: like "see"
na: na: like "nah"
ah: rhymes with singing "la!"
Ha: like laughing "ha!"
nis: like "niece"
ta: tah as in "Utah"
ret: *reht* as in "**ret**ina"

Le-ra-ye She-me-o-rer Sa-fek
Zepar Shel Ha-sod Ve-ha-yi-rah
O-ro-bas Ha-si-na-ah Ha-nis-ta-ret

Persistent Nightmares

Invade the sleep of your target, ensuring they experience relentless, terrifying dreams. Create a nightly hell that leaves them exhausted, fearful, and mentally fragile. The nightmares are vivid and horrifying, haunting their every slumber and making restful sleep impossible.

Imagine a high-powered lawyer who thrives on their sharp mind and quick wit. With this ritual, their nights become a battlefield of grotesque visions and relentless fears. They wake up drenched in sweat, unable to shake the images from their dreams. Their performance at work declines as exhaustion and fear replace confidence and precision. The once formidable attorney becomes a shadow of their former self, haunted by the horrors that greet them every night.

Or think of a socialite who's always the life of the party, exuding charm and confidence. As the magick takes hold, their nights are filled with terror, and their days with the lingering dread of sleep. The socialite's sparkle fades, replaced by dark circles and a pervasive sense of anxiety. Social gatherings become unbearable, and their once vibrant presence is overshadowed by the fear of what awaits them in their sleep.

The power of the ritual lies in its ability to erode the target's mental and physical health gradually but surely. Night after night, the relentless nightmares sap their strength, making it harder for them to function during the day. The target becomes increasingly paranoid and fearful, struggling to distinguish between dream and reality.

Demons to Invoke

Morax: Known for creating fear and terror, Morax can ensure the target's sleep is filled with vivid, horrifying nightmares that leave them mentally and physically exhausted.

Asmodai: Specialises in twisting desires and causing uncontrollable urges. Asmodai can manipulate dreams to amplify the target's deepest fears, turning their sleep into a nightly ordeal.

Forneus: Known for creating confusion among enemies, Forneus can invade the target's dreams, causing them to experience chaotic and disturbing nightmares that disrupt their sleep and peace of mind.

Words of Power for Persistent Nightmares

As-mo-dai Ha-ma-yim Ha-a-fe-lim

As: rhymes with "jazz"
mo: like "maw"
dai: like "dye"
Ha: like laughing "ha!"
ma: *mah* as in "ma**ma**"
yim: *yeem* rhymes with "ream"
Ha: like laughing "ha!"
a: rhymes with singing "la!"
fe: *feh* as in "**fe**d"
lim: starts with *l* and rhymes with "ream"

Mo-rax Be-tza-a-kot

Mo: like "maw"
rax: like "rucks"
Beh: *beh* as in "**be**t"
Tza: as in "**Tsar**- a cross between "star" and "char"
a: rhymes with singing "la!"
kot: like "cot"

For-ne-us Shel Ha-lai-la Le-lo She-na

For: like "four"
ne: *neh* as in "**ne**t"
us: *uss* as in "cuss"
Shel: like "shell"
Ha: like laughing "ha!"

lai: like "lie"
la: like singing "la!"
Le: *leh* as in "**let**"
lo: like "law"
She: *sheh* as in "**she**d"
na: like "nah"

As-mo-dai Ha-ma-yim Ha-a-fe-lim
Mo-rax Be-tza-a-kot
For-ne-us Shel Ha-lai-la Le-lo She-na

Career Collapse

A thriving career can be the cornerstone of a person's identity and self-worth. The Career Collapse ritual aims to dismantle this pillar, causing professional ruin and public disgrace. It can ruin reputation, opportunities, and confidence, leaving their career in tatters.

Imagine the ambitious manager climbing the corporate ladder, confident and untouchable. As this ritual takes effect, their decisions backfire spectacularly. Projects fail, crucial deals fall through, and their colleagues turn against them. Whispers of incompetence spread, and before long, the once-promising career is in freefall, leaving them scrambling to salvage their reputation.

Then there's the well-respected professor who prides herself on her achievements and influence. As the curse unfolds, her research is discredited, her lectures become erratic, and students lose respect. Colleagues begin to distance themselves, and academic opportunities dry up. Her confidence erodes, and she watches helplessly as her career crumbles around her.

The ritual undermines every aspect of the target's professional life, ensuring a complete and humiliating downfall.

Demons to Invoke

Agares: Specialises in ruining reputations and stimulating decision and action. Agares can make the target act impulsively and unwisely, leading to professional blunders and public humiliation.

Eligos: Known for knowing enemy plans and causing blind affection, Eligos can manipulate the target's professional relationships, leading to betrayals, misunderstandings, and a loss of support from colleagues and superiors.

Barbatos: Capable of revealing secrets and gaining respect, Barbatos can inversely ensure the target's hidden flaws and mistakes are exposed, leading to a loss of respect and credibility in their professional field.

Words of Power for Career Collapse

A-ga-res Ko-fetz Me-ha-ma-tzok

A: rhymes with singing "la!"
ga: *ga* as in "ga**ga**"
res: *rez* as in "**res**erve"
Ko: like "caw"
fetz: *fet* as in "**fet**ter" but ends with *tzuh* sound
me: *meh* as in "**met**"
ha: like laughing "ha!"
ma: *mah* as in "ma**ma**"
tzok: starts with *tz* sound- a cross between "stock" and "choc"

E-li-gos La-a-sot Sho-teh

Eh: *eh* as in "**e**lf"
li: *lee* as in "**lea**n"
gos: like "gauze"
La: like singing "la!"
a: rhymes with singing "la!"
sot: *sot* as in "be**sot**"
Sho: *shaw* as in "rick**shaw**"
teh: *teh* as in "**te**pid"

Bar-ba-tos Li-dros Et

Bar: like "bar"
ba: *bah* as in "ba**ba**"
tos: like "taws"
Li: *lee* as in "**lea**n"

dros: like "drawers"
Et: *eht* as in "**et**iqu**ett**e"

A-ga-res Ko-fetz Me-ha-ma-tzok
E-li-gos La-a-sot Sho-teh
Bar-ba-tos Li-dros Et

Health Hex

Health is a fragile thing, and the Health Hex is a ritual designed to exploit that fragility, inflicting illness and chronic health issues on a targeted individual. This hex doesn't just cause temporary discomfort; it brings about sustained suffering and disrupts the target's physical well-being.

Think about the fitness enthusiast who prides themselves on their health and vitality. As this hex takes hold, they start experiencing unexplained fatigue, persistent aches, and recurring illnesses. Their once-active lifestyle becomes a struggle, and they find themselves increasingly confined to bed rest, watching their health deteriorate.

Or consider the vibrant socialite who thrives on being the centre of attention. As the ritual works its dark magick, they develop chronic health issues that make socialising impossible. Frequent doctor's visits, medications, and treatments become their new reality. Their energy drains away, leaving them isolated and struggling to maintain their social standing.

The Health Hex is relentless, causing ongoing physical distress that disrupts every aspect of the target's life. You can significantly disrupt a person's physical well-being, leaving them vulnerable and preoccupied with their health problems.

Demons to Invoke

Vepar: Specialises in infecting to make weak and increasing sickness. Vepar can induce severe and persistent illnesses that undermine the target's physical health and vitality.

Marbas: Known for casting infections and curing infections, Marbas can be invoked to cause stubborn infections that are resistant to treatment, leading to chronic health problems.

Sabnock: Capable of causing exhaustion and delusions, Sabnock can ensure the target experiences debilitating fatigue and health issues that disrupt their daily life and social activities.

Words of Power for the Health Hex

Ve-par Li-grom Khul-sha

Ve: *veh* as in "**vet**"
par: like "par"
Li: *lee* as in "**lea**n"
grom: *grawm* as in "po**grom**"
Khul: starts with trilled *k* and rhymes with "cool"
sha: like "Shah"

Mar-bas Shel Ba-sar Ra-kuv

Mar: like "mar"
bas: starts with *b* and rhymes with "jazz"
Shel: like "shell"
ba: *bah* as in "ba**ba**"
sar: *sar* as in "**sar**i"
Ra: *rah* as in "**ra**men"
kuv: starts with *k* and rhymes with "move"

Sab-nok Me-ta-yesh Ha-sha-ma-yim

Sab: like "Saab"
nok: like "knock"
Me: *meh* as in "**met**"
ta: tah as in "U**tah**"
yesh: starts with *y* and rhymes with "mesh"
Ha: like laughing "ha!"
sha: like "Shah"
ma: *mah* as in "ma**ma**"
yim: *yeem* rhymes with "ream"

Ve-par Li-grom Khul-sha
Mar-bas Shel Ba-sar Ra-kuv
Sab-nok Me-ta-yesh Ha-sha-ma-yim

Family Feud

While this power sounds like the title of a 70s TV gameshow, it is anything but mild. With this power, you can summon conflict and tension to emerge within a family, causing rifts, estrangement, and utterly broken relationships. This isn't about a minor argument; it's about creating deep-seated animosity that tears families apart. It's like planting seeds of discord that grow into thorny bushes, making family harmony impossible.

Do you have a family that's always bragging about their closeness? Use Family Feud and watch as their bonds start to fray. Small disagreements turn into explosive fights, secrets come to light, and trust evaporates. They go from being a united front to a fractured mess, with members taking sides and holding grudges.

Or think of a family that's always sticking together against you. After the ritual, old wounds resurface, and new conflicts arise. Family gatherings become battlegrounds, with everyone too focused on their own grievances to support each other. The once-solid family unit dissolves into a chaotic tangle of resentments and accusations.

Family Feud is like introducing a virus into the family dynamic, one that spreads and causes lasting damage to their relationships.

Demons to Invoke

Botis: Specialises in reading thoughts and feelings and causing disfigurement, Botis can reveal hidden resentments and amplify misunderstandings, leading to explosive fights and long-lasting grudges.

Leraye: Known for causing conflict, Leraye will find the best opportunities to create problems.

Foras: With the power to conceal the valuable and induce forgetfulness, Foras can hide the family's sense of unity and trust, leading to estrangement and broken relationships.

Words of Power for Family Feud

Bo-tis Le-a-vot Ha-pa-nim

Bo: *baw* as in "**baw**l"
tis: *tis* as in "no**tice**"
Le: *leh* as in "**let**"
a: rhymes with singing "la!"
vot: *vot* as in "ga**vot**te"
Ha: like laughing "ha!"
pa: *pah* as in "Pa**pa**"
nim: starts with *n* and rhymes with "meme"

Le-ra-ye La-a-sot Kol Ha-o-y-vim Le-ha-ir

Le: *leh* as in "**let**"
ra: *rah* as in "**ra**men"
ye: *yeh* as in "**yet**"
La: like singing "la!"
a: rhymes with singing "la!"
sot: *sot* as in "be**sot**"
Kol: like "coal"
Ha: like laughing "ha!"
o: like "awe"
y: starts with *y* as in "**yu**ck" and rhymes with "duh"
vim: starts with *v* and rhymes with "beam"
Le: *leh* as in "**let**"
ha: like laughing "ha!"
ir: like "ear"

For: like "four"
ras: *raz* rhymes with "jazz"
Ha: like laughing "ha!"
sho: *shaw* as in "rick**shaw**"
ver: *vehr* as in "**ver**y"

Bo-tis Le-a-vot Ha-pa-nim
Le-ra-ye La-a-sot Kol Ha-o-y-vim Le-ha-ir
Fo-ras Ha-sho-ver

Social Isolation

Humans are social creatures, and the Social Isolation ritual is designed to strip away this essential aspect of life, leaving the target lonely and vulnerable. This ritual manipulates social dynamics to cut the target off from friends, family, and their community. It's like building an invisible wall around them, keeping everyone else out.

Anybody who's popular or who thrives on constant attention and adoration is a perfect victim. As the ritual sets in, their followers begin to unfollow, friends drift away, and invitations dry up. Their presence dwindles, and they find themselves increasingly alone, struggling to understand what went wrong. The ritual is merciless, ensuring that the target is left to face their loneliness with no support or companionship.

When you have a colleague who's too popular for their own good, use this and watch as their social circle starts to shrink. Friends become distant, and their once-busy social life turns into a series of lonely weekends with no one to turn to.

Or what about a man who uses social standing and connections to enable abuse of his partner and children? Or 'pillar of the community' types who everyone supports even after child sexual abuse allegations? Taking action against these people can be satisfying and stops them from getting away with their crimes.

Social Isolation is like pulling the social safety net out from under someone, leaving them to fall into the void of loneliness.

Demons to Invoke

Raum: Known for causing mistrust, Raum can create an atmosphere of suspicion around the target, making friends and acquaintances doubt their intentions and gradually distance themselves.

Gusoin: Specialises in loosening tongues and bringing respect. By using this power inversely, Gusoin can cause secrets and gossip to spread, leading to the target's social downfall and isolation.

Barbatos: Specialises in revealing secrets and gaining intuition. Barbatos can bring hidden issues to light, causing conflicts and misunderstandings that lead to the target being ostracised by their social circle.

Words of Power for Social Isolation

Ra-um Sho-mer Ha-she-ker

Ra: *rah* as in "**ra**men"
um: *oom* as in "**room**"
Sho: *shaw* as in "rick**shaw**"
mer: *mehr* as in "**mer**ry"
Ha: like laughing "ha!"
She: *sheh* as in "**she**d"
ker: *kehr* as in "**ker**osene"

Gu-so-in Me-vi Tza-ar Ga-dol

Gu: *goo* as in "**goo**ey"
so: Like "saw"
in: *een* as in "**een**y"
Me: *meh* as in "**me**t"
vi: *vee* as in "**Ve**nus"
Tza: as in "Tsar- a cross between "star" and "char"
ar: *ahr* as in "**ar**rest"
Ga: *ga* as in "ga**ga**"
dol: like "doll"

Bar-ba-tos Shel Ha-ne-ka-ma Ha-so-dit

Bar: like "bar"
ba: *bah* as in "ba**ba**"
tos: like "taws"
Shel: like "shell"
Ha: like laughing "ha!"
ne: *neh* as in "**ne**t"

ka: kah as in "**cup**"
ma: *mah* as in "ma**ma**"
Ha: like laughing "ha!"
so: Like "saw"
dit: *dee* as in "**det**ox"

Ra-um Sho-mer Ha-she-ker
Gu-so-in Me-vi Tza-ar Ga-dol
Bar-ba-tos Shel Ha-ne-ka-ma Ha-so-dit

Sleep Disturbance

Sleep is essential for well-being, and the Sleep Disturbance ritual aims to disrupt this crucial aspect of life, causing insomnia and exhaustion. This ritual ensures that the target is deprived of restful sleep, leading to physical and mental deterioration.

Imagine the overachiever who relies on a strict sleep schedule to maintain peak performance. As this ritual takes effect, they find themselves tossing and turning, unable to fall asleep. When they do manage to drift off, their sleep is plagued by anxiety. Their once-sharp mind becomes foggy, and their performance suffers as exhaustion takes its toll.

Or think of a neighbour who's always causing trouble. After the ritual, they find it impossible to get a good night's rest. Every sound wakes them up, and their dreams are filled with disturbing images. They become too exhausted to keep up their usual antics, retreating into their home in a state of perpetual fatigue. Do not use this if the neighbour ever complains about the noise you make, or they will blame you. Otherwise, you'll be fine.

Demons to Invoke

Morax: Known for creating fear and confusion, Morax can induce vivid nightmares that plague the target's sleep, leading to exhaustion and mental strain.

Foras: Specialises in causing forgetfulness and mental disarray. Foras can disrupt the target's ability to fall asleep and stay asleep, leading to insomnia and mental fog.

Furfur: Specialises in causing electrical disturbances and anger. Furfur can induce a state of restlessness and irritability, ensuring the target's sleep is constantly disrupted by minor disturbances and mental turmoil.

Words of Power for Sleep Disturbance

Mo-rax Lai-la Ha-ei-ma

Mo: like "maw"
rax: like "rucks"
Lai: like "lie"
la: like singing "la!"
Ha: like laughing "ha!"
ei: *ehyi* as in "**ai**m"
ma: *mah* as in "ma**ma**"

Fo-ras Shel Da-at To-eh

For: like "four"
ras: *raz* rhymes with "jazz"
Shel: like "shell"
Da: *dah* as in "**dah**l"
at: *aht* as in "bh**at**"
To: like "taw"
eh: *eh* as in "**e**lf"

Fur-fur Ni-tzo-tzot Shel Za-am

Fur: like "fur"
fur: like "Fur"
Ni: like "knee"
tzo: starts with *tz* sound- a cross between "store" and "chaw"
tzot: starts with *tz* sound-cross between "stoat" and "chort"
Shel: like "shell"
Za: *zah* as in "huz**zah**!"

am: like "I **am**"

Mo-rax Lai-la Ha-ei-ma
Fo-ras Shel Da-at To-eh
Fur-fur Ni-tzo-tzot Shel Za-am

Identity Theft

Identity Theft is a ritual designed to leave someone vulnerable to modern privacy disruption, from password theft and scams to complete identity destruction. It can throw a person's entire sense of self and financial stability into chaos. It's like planting a time bomb in their digital life, set to detonate and cause widespread havoc.

Think of a rival who's too confident in their digital security. Use Identity Theft and watch as their online world starts to crumble. They might find their email hacked, their social media accounts compromised, and their financial information stolen. Their attempts to reclaim their identity turn into a frustrating maze of bureaucratic red tape and mounting losses.

Or think of someone who's always boasting about their online prowess. After the ritual, they start receiving fraudulent charges, their credit score plummets, and they find themselves caught in a web of scams. Their digital reputation is tarnished, and their personal information is scattered across the internet, causing endless headaches and financial woes.

Demons to Invoke

Agares: Specialises in ruining reputations and causing hesitation. Agares can manipulate the target's digital footprint, making it easy for hackers to exploit their personal information and financial data.

Glasya-Labolas: Known for causing sickness and provoking attacks, Glasya-Labolas can incite targeted cyber-attacks and scams, ensuring the target's digital identity is thoroughly exploited.

Ronove: Specialises in improving charisma and causing disloyalty. Ronove can manipulate the target's social connections, making it easier for impostors to assume their identity and damage their reputation.

Words of Power for Identity Theft

A-ga-res Me-vi Ha-re-ga

A: rhymes with singing "la!"
ga: *gah* as in "ga**ga**"
res: *rez* as in "**res**erve"
Me: *meh* as in "**me**t"
vi: *vee* as in "**V**enus"
Ha: like laughing "ha!"
re: *reh* as in "**re**d"
ga: *gah* as in "ga**ga**"

Gla-sya La-bo-las Maz-min O-tam Knee-ma

Gla: *glah* as in "**gla**cé"
Suh: starts with *s* as in "**su**p" and rhymes with "duh"
Yuh: starts with *y* as in "**yu**ck" and rhymes with "duh"
A: rhymes with singing "la!"
La: like singing "la!"
Bo: *baw* as in "**baw**l"
las: *laz* as in "**lais**sez faire"
Maz: like "muzz"
min: like "mean"
O: like "awe"
tam: *tam* as in "**tam**p"
Kuh: starts with *k* and rhymes with "duh"
Nee: like "knee"
ma: *mah* as in "ma**ma**"

Ro-no-ve Ha-bo-ged

Ro: like "raw"

no: like "gnaw"
ve: *veh* as in "**vet**"
Ha: like laughing "ha!"
Bo: *baw* as in "**bawl**"
ged: *ged* as in "rug**ged**" and rhymes with "get"

A-ga-res Me-vi Ha-re-ga
Gla-sya La-bo-las Maz-min O-tam Knee-ma
Ro-no-ve Ha-bo-ged

Legal Disarray

Legal Disarray is a ritual designed to manipulate legal proceedings, causing chaos and confusion to gain an advantage. It's like throwing a wrench into the cogs of the justice system, ensuring that nothing runs smoothly.

If you have an adversary who's tied up in a legal battle use Legal Disarray and watch as their case becomes a tangled mess. They might face sudden delays, lose crucial evidence, or encounter unexpected legal challenges. Their lawyers become ineffective, and the court seems to turn against them, leaving them trapped in a frustrating and costly legal quagmire.

Or think of someone who's always quick to sue or threaten legal action. After the ritual, their legal threats start to backfire. Cases they thought were airtight begin to crumble, judges rule against them, and their legal team struggles to keep up. They become entangled in legal issues that drain their resources and damage their reputation.

Demons to Invoke

Vine: Specialises in breaking the will of mercenaries and discovering disloyal thieves. Vine can manipulate legal proceedings to exploit loopholes, cause mistrust among legal teams, and ensure that key players become unreliable.

Forneus: Capable of causing confusion and making enemies fear you, Forneus can manipulate the target's legal adversaries to act irrationally, leading to miscommunications and poorly executed legal manoeuvres.

Sabnock: Known for causing delusions and exhaustion, Sabnock can induce mental strain and confusion in the target and their legal team, leading to errors, misjudgements, and a general state of disarray.

Words of Power for Legal Disarray

Vine She-sho-ver Ha-ra-tzon

Vi: *vee* as in "**Ve**nus"
ne: *neh* as in "**net**"
She: *sheh* as in "**she**d"
sho: *shaw* as in "rick**shaw**"
ver: *vehr* as in "**ver**y"
Ha: like laughing "ha!"
ra: *rah* as in "**ra**men"
tzon: starts with *tz* sound- a cross between "stone and "chawn"

For-ne-us Shel Ha-a-nan

For: like "four"
ne: *neh* as in "**net**"
us: *uss* as in "cuss"
Shel: like "shell"
Ha: like laughing "ha!"
a: rhymes with singing "la!"
nan: like "naan"

Sab-nok Mat-nat Ha-ash-la-ya

Sab: like "Saab"
nok: like "knock"
Mat: *maht* as in "stig**mat**a"
nat: *naht* as in "so**nat**a"
Ha: like laughing "ha!"
ash: *ahsh* as in "**ush**er"
la: like singing "la!"

ya: *yah* as in "**yu**m"

Vine She-sho-ver Ha-ra-tzon
For-ne-us Shel Ha-a-nan
Sab-nok Mat-nat Ha-ash-la-ya

Memory Implantation

This is a deeply insidious ritual designed to implant false memories into a person's mind. The havoc this can wreak is beyond belief, as the target's perception of reality is slowly and meticulously altered. It's not about immediate chaos but a slow, creeping manipulation that reshapes their history and identity.

Consider the meticulous accountant who relies on a flawless memory for their work. As the ritual takes hold, they start to recall events that never happened, making critical errors in their calculations. They argue with colleagues about things they remember clearly, but that never occurred. Over time, their credibility erodes, and they are seen as unreliable.

Or picture the devoted parent whose life revolves around their children's milestones. As the implanted memories take root, they begin to recall fabricated incidents, creating confusion and distrust within the family. They insist on memories that never existed, causing rifts and emotional pain. Their sense of reality becomes distorted, and their relationships suffer.

The beauty of Memory Implantation lies in its subtlety and its power to alter the target's very sense of self and reality, creating a foundation of falsehoods that undermine their confidence and trust. You do not get to choose what memories are implanted. Trust that the demons will choose wisely.

Demons to Invoke

Vassago: Known for discovering truth and knowing the past, Vassago can twist these abilities to implant false memories, causing the target to recall events that never happened, leading to confusion and errors.

Gaap: With the power to create drowsiness and foggy thoughts, Gaap can manipulate the target's mind to accept and reinforce false memories, making them indistinguishable from real ones.

Balam: Capable of reducing attention and presence, Balam can distract the target's mental focus, making it easier to implant and reinforce false memories without their awareness.

Words of Power for Memory Implantation

Va-sa-go Shel Ha-da-at Ha-she-krit

Vah: *vah* as in "**va**ledictory"
sah: *sah* as in "**su**n"
goh: like "Go"
Shel: like "shell"
Ha: like laughing "ha!"
da: *dah* as in "**dah**l"
at: *aht* as in "bh**at**"
Ha: like laughing "ha!"
She: *sheh* as in "**she**d"
krit: like "Crete"

Ga-ap Ha-mat-eh Ha-ya-shen

Ga: *ga* as in "ga**ga**"
ap: *ahp* as in "**ap**ply"
Ha: like laughing "ha!"
mat: *maht* as in "stig**mat**a"
eh: *eh* as in "**e**lf"
Ha: like laughing "ha!"
ya: *yah* as in "**yu**m"
shen: *shen* as in "**shen**anigan"

Ba-lam Ha-ha-sa-kha

Ba: *bah* as in "ba**ba**"
lam: Like "lamb"
Ha: like laughing "ha!"
ha: like laughing "ha!"
sa: *sah* as in "**su**n"

kha: starts with coughed *k* and rhymes with "ha!"

Va-sa-go Shel Ha-da-at Ha-she-krit
Ga-ap Ha-mat-eh Ha-ya-shen
Ba-lam Ha-ha-sa-kha

Emotional Destruction

Emotional Destruction is a ritual that targets the core of a person's emotional stability, inducing mood swings. It's like flipping a switch in someone's mind, causing their emotions to run wild and out of control.

Have you got an opponent who's always calm and collected? Use Emotional Destruction and watch them unravel. They might go from anger to despair in a matter of minutes, lashing out at those around them. Their relationships suffer as friends and family struggle to deal with their erratic behaviour. At work, their inability to maintain composure leads to conflicts and poor decisions, ultimately affecting their professional reputation.

Or consider that annoying neighbour who's always cheerful and peppy. After the ritual, their mood takes a nosedive. They become prone to fits of rage or deep bouts of sadness, alienating those around them. Their constant mood swings make it impossible for anyone to be around them for long, leaving them isolated and distraught.

Demons to Invoke

Gaap: Specialises in creating arguments and irrational lust. Gaap can manipulate the target's emotions, causing them to swing wildly between extremes, leading to emotional instability and irrational actions.

Vepar: Capable of subduing the proud and causing infection, Vepar can induce a state of emotional turmoil, leading to intense feelings of insecurity, agitation, and emotional instability.

Marchosias: Specialises in dissuading enemies and negotiating forcefully. Marchosias can corrupt the target's emotional stability, causing them to experience intense emotional swings and irrational behaviour.

Words of Power for Emotional Destruction

Mar-ko-si-as She-mar-pe Et Ha-metzi-ut

March: like "mark" but ends with hard *h*/soft *k* sound
o: like "awe"
si: like "see"
as: rhymes with "jazz"
She: *sheh* as in "**she**d"
Mar: like "mar"
pe: *peh* as in "**pe**t"
Et: *eht* as in "**et**ique**tt**e"
Ha: like laughing "ha!"
Me: me: *meh* as in "**me**t"
Tzi: starts with *tz* sound- a cross between "stee" and "chee"
ut: *oot* as in "h**oot**"

Ga-ap Ha-e-mun Ha-sha-vur

Ga: *ga* as in "ga**ga**"
ap: *ahp* as in "**ap**ply"
Ha: like laughing "ha!"
eh: *eh* as in "**el**f"
mun: like "moon"
Ha: like laughing "ha!"
sha: like "Shah"
vur: *vur* as in "**ver**se"

Ve-par Ha-da-at Ha-ra-ku-va

Ve: *veh* as in "**ve**t"
par: like "par"

Ha: like laughing "ha!"
da: *dah* as in "**dah**l"
at: *aht* as in "bh**at**"
Ha: like laughing "ha!"
Ra: *rah* as in "**ra**men"
ku: like "coup"
vah: *vah* as in "**va**ledictory"

Mar-ko-si-as She-mar-pe Et Ha-metzi-ut
Ga-ap Ha-e-mun Ha-sha-vur
Ve-par Ha-da-at Ha-ra-ku-va

Property Curse

The Property Curse is designed to bring misfortune to someone's possessions, causing accidents, disasters, and financial loss. This ritual aims to systematically destroy the target's property, turning their assets into liabilities and their peace of mind into a state of constant worry.

When somebody is always bragging about their pristine house, use this and watch their home become a source of constant trouble. Pipes burst unexpectedly, electrical problems arise, and appliances break down repeatedly. Their once-perfect home becomes a money pit, draining their finances and patience.

Or what about that coworker who's always flaunting their expensive car? After the ritual, their prized vehicle starts having mysterious issues. Engine trouble, flat tyres, and unexplained damages leave them stranded and frustrated. The cost of repairs adds up, and their confidence takes a hit as their symbol of success becomes a source of stress.

Demons to Invoke

Forcalor: Known for causing persistent sickness and business failure, Forcalor can extend his influence to create continuous problems and accidents with the target's property, leading to financial strain and constant repairs.

Vepar: Capable of causing infection and increasing sickness, Vepar can ensure the target's property, such as their garden or home, is plagued by pests and infestations, causing significant damage and expense.

Sabnock: Known for causing delusions and exhaustion, Sabnock can induce a state where the target's property continually deteriorates, causing them to spend excessive amounts on repairs and maintenance.

Words of Power for the Property Curse

For-ca-lor Shel Ha-sha-vur

For: like "four"
cal: starts with *k* and rhymes with "gull"
or: *aur* as in "**aur**a"
Shel: like "shell"
Ha: like laughing "ha!"
sha: like "Shah"
vur: *vur* as in "**ver**se"

Ve-par Ha-ba-yit Ha-na-fol

Ve: *veh* as in "**vet**"
par: like "par"
Ha: like laughing "ha!"
ba: *bah* as in "ba**ba**"
yit: like "yeet"
Ha: like laughing "ha!"
na: like "nah"
fol: like "foal"

Sab-nok Ha-shich-no-a Ha-ein So-fi

Sab: like "Saab"
nok: like "knock"
Ha: like laughing "ha!"
shich: like "Sheik" but ends with hard *h*/soft *k* sound
no: like "gnaw"
a: rhymes with singing "la!"
Ha: like laughing "ha!"
ein: *ehyeen* as in "v**ein**"

So: Like "saw"
fi: like "fee"

For-ca-lor Shel Ha-sha-vur
Ve-par Ha-ba-yit Ha-na-fol
Sab-nok Ha-shich-no-a Ha-ein So-fi

Social Media Sabotage

In the age of digital presence, a person's reputation on social media can be everything. The curse is designed to tarnish this reputation by spreading rumours, misinformation, and causing relationships to fracture.

When you have a rival who's popular online, the best way to hurt them is to sabotage their online world. Fake accounts start spreading damaging rumours, their posts attract negative attention, and their follower count drops. Friends and followers begin to doubt their credibility, and their once-polished image becomes a battleground of accusations and controversies.

Or think of a colleague who's always boasting about their social media influence. After the ritual, their account gets hacked, private messages get leaked, and they're caught in a web of online scandals. Their professional and personal life takes a hit as their digital footprint turns from a source of pride to a source of shame. It can work more imaginatively as well, leading to unexpected leaks of photographs.

Demons to Invoke

Forneus: Known for causing confusion and manipulating perceptions, Forneus can spread misinformation and rumours, leading to the target's reputation being severely damaged.

Belial: Specialises in causing chaos and disruption. Belial can ensure that the target's social media presence is plagued with doctored photos, misinterpreted posts, and leaked private messages, leading to a public scandal.

Raum: Specialises in causing mistrust and sowing discord. Raum can manipulate social media interactions to create conflicts and misunderstandings, leading to fractured relationships and a tarnished reputation.

Words of Power for Social Media Sabotage

For-ne-us To-fes Ha-yi-ra

For: like "four"
ne: *neh* as in "**ne**t"
us: *uss* as in "cuss"
To: like "taw"
fes: like "fez"
Ha: like laughing "ha!"
yi: *yee* as in "**yee**ha!"
ra: *rah* as in "**ra**men"

Be-li-al Ha-mi-lim Ha-ka-o-ti-yot

Beh: *beh* as in "**bet**"
li: *lee* as in "**lea**n"
al: rhymes with "gull"
Ha: like laughing "ha!"
mi: like the pronoun "me"
lim: starts with *l* and rhymes with "ream"
Ha: like laughing "ha!"
ka: kah as in "**cu**p"
o: like "awe"
ti: like "tea"
yot: starts with *y* and rhymes with "jot"

Ra-um A-vur Bu-sha Sha-cho-ra

Ra: *rah* as in "**ra**men"
um: *oom* as in "**room**"
A: rhymes with singing "la!"
vur: *vur* as in "**ver**se"

Bu: like "Boo!"
sha: like "Shah"
Sha: like "Shah"
cho: like "caw" but starts with hard *h*/soft *k* sound
ra: *rah* as in "**ra**men"

For-ne-us To-fes Ha-yi-ra
Be-li-al Ha-mi-lim Ha-ka-o-ti-yot
Ra-um A-vur Bu-sha Sha-cho-ra

Addiction Enchantment

This curse can have long-lasting effects because you can enchant an enemy to become addicted to harmful substances or behaviours. You will create a deep-seated dependency that wrecks their life. Addiction is like a parasite that gnaws away at their self-control and well-being.

When you have an enemy that you truly want to destroy, this is the finest way to do so. Use this curse, and they will spiral into destructive habits. They might develop a dependence on alcohol, drugs, or gambling; you don't need to decide. The demons will know what will cause the most damage. The person who once seemed invincible becomes a shadow of their former self, and the effects can last for the rest of their time on earth.

Avoid this ritual if the addictive behaviours could cause harm to other people that you care about, and ensure you are at a distance. You wouldn't set off a firework in your own home, and it's obvious you don't want an addict there either. This is so obvious it barely needs stating.

Demons to Invoke

Asmodai: Known for twisting desires and causing uncontrollable urges, Asmodai can create powerful addictions that consume the target's life, leading them into destructive behaviours.

Zepar: Known for influencing love and sexual attraction, Zepar can twist these abilities to make the target develop addictions, turning harmless interests into life-consuming obsessions.

Botis: Capable of reading thoughts and feelings, Botis can implant the seeds of addiction in the target's mind, making them gradually succumb to their desires and lose control over their actions.

Words of Power for the Addiction Enchantment

As-mo-dai A-vur Tza-me Za-am

As: rhymes with "jazz"
mo: like "maw"
dai: like "dye"
A: rhymes with singing "la!"
vur: *vur* as in "**ver**se"
Tza: as in "Tsar- a cross between "star" and "char"
me: me: *meh* as in "**me**t"
Za: *zah* as in "huz**zah**!"
am: like "I **am**"

Ze-par A-vur Ta-a-va Knee-mit

Ze: *zeh* as in "**ze**nith"
par: like "par"
A: rhymes with singing "la!"
vur: *vur* as in "**ver**se"
Ta: tah as in "U**tah**"
a: rhymes with singing "la!"
va: *vah* as in "**va**ledictory"
Kuh: starts with *k* and rhymes with "duh"
nee: like "knee"
mit: like "meet"

Bo-tis Mach-zir Et Ha-ma-a-gal Shel Ra-a-yon

Bo: *baw* as in "**baw**l"
tis: *tis* as in "no**tice**"
Mach: like "muck" but ends with hard *h*/soft *k* sound

zir: starts with *z* and rhymes with "steer"
Et: *eht* as in "**et**ique**tt**e"
Ha: like laughing "ha!"
ma: *mah* as in "ma**ma**"
a: rhymes with singing "la!"
gal: like "gull"
Shel: like "shell"
Ra: *rah* as in "**ra**men"
a: rhymes with singing "la!"
yon: like "yawn"

As-mo-dai A-vur Tza-me Za-am
Ze-par A-vur Ta-a-va Knee-mit
Bo-tis Mach-zir Et Ha-ma-a-gal
Shel Ra-a-yon

Psychic Turbulence

Create psychic turbulence around a person, disrupting their thoughts, feelings, and mental stability through a fear of the paranormal. This works best on people who already believe or suspect that the paranormal is dangerous. Used against religious types, it's bliss.

You can use this when you want your victim to experience extreme fear with a hint of guilt. For whatever reason, this curse makes people believe that they have brought on the chaos. They may even feel that they deserve this punishment. They might start experiencing intrusive thoughts, emotional swings, and an inability to focus as they overreact to sounds, imagined shadows, and creeping dread. Their decisions become erratic, and their interactions with others are fraught with tension.

Apply this ritual when you know the person could easily believe in the paranormal and when you want them to experience unexplained guilt.

Demons to Invoke

Marbas: Specialises in causing illness and healing. Marbas can disrupt the target's mental clarity, leading to anxiety, confusion, and an inability to focus.

Forneus: Known for creating confusion and fear, Forneus can manipulate the target's emotions and thoughts, causing a constant state of psychic turbulence and mental chaos.

Gaap: Specialises in creating irrational lust and hatred. Gaap can introduce chaotic thoughts and emotions, making it difficult for the target to maintain mental and emotional stability.

Words of Power for Psychic Turbulence

Mar-bas Ha-da-at Ha-so-rer-et

Mar: like "mar"
bas: starts with *b* and rhymes with "jazz"
Ha: like laughing "ha!"
da: *dah* as in "**dah**l"
at: *aht* as in "bh**at**"
Ha: like laughing "ha!"
so: Like "saw"
rer: like "rare"
et: *eht* as in "**et**ique**tte**"

For-ne-us A-vur Gal Pni-mi Shel Ge-shem

For: like "four"
ne: *neh* as in "**net**"
us: *uss* as in "cuss"
A: rhymes with singing "la!"
vur: *vur* as in "**ver**se"
Gal: like "gull"
Puh: starts with *p* and rhymes with "duh"
ni: like "knee"
mi: like the pronoun "me"
Shel: like "shell"
Ge: *geh* as in "**get**"
shem: *shem* as in "**shem**ozzle"

Ga-ap A-vur Ri-fyon

Ga: *ga* as in "ga**ga**"
ap: *ahp* as in "**ap**ply"

A: rhymes with singing "la!"
vur: *vur* as in "**ver**se"
Ri: *ree* as in "**ree**d"
fuh: starts with *f* and rhymes with "duh"
yon: like "yawn"

Mar-bas Ha-da-at Ha-so-rer-et
For-ne-us A-vur Gal Pni-mi Shel Ge-shem
Ga-ap A-vur Ri-fyon

Disruptive Weather

Weather magick is unreliable, at best. You're fighting the reality of many people when you try to change the weather. Usually, it doesn't work very well unless you have a good reason. There are many sailors who use magick and swear by it, but I've never been convinced that you can ask for clear weather for your summer vacation. If you want to cause harm, the weather can respond to demons.

If there's an event you want to ruin, you can watch as the skies darken and a storm rolls in. Weddings, outdoor concerts, or important meetings get washed out by torrential rain or disrupted by sudden snowstorms. The meticulous plans of your target are thrown into chaos, leaving them scrambling to cope with the natural disaster. This is one curse where you can turn up and watch the events unfold, so long as you take real-world precautions.

When a business relies on good weather, you can do great harm. You are more likely to get a result if you are aiming to spoil one day rather than a whole month.

Magick that affects the weather is uncommon in modern magick books largely because it's not very good but also because it seems unbelievable, and not many people want to admit that it works. The texts and manuals that contain the oldest magick are full of rituals for the weather because it was such an important part of everyone's life before we found a way to shield ourselves from the outdoors most of the time. You should get results that convince you this is real.

Demons to Invoke

Vepar: Specialises in causing rain and sea storms. Vepar can ensure torrential downpours, floods, and chaotic sea conditions, leading to widespread disruption and chaos.

Amdusias: Amdusias can invoke severe weather conditions, such as thunderstorms and strong winds, to disrupt events and daily life.

Buer: Known for influencing natural elements, Buer can manipulate weather patterns to create unexpected snowstorms, heatwaves, or other extreme weather conditions, causing significant inconvenience and disruption.

Words of Power for Disruptive Weather

Ve-par Shel Ha-se-a-ra Ha-do-mem-et

Ve: *veh* as in "**ve**t"
par: like "par"
Shel: like "shell"
Ha: like laughing "ha!"
se: *seh* as in "**se**t"
a: rhymes with singing "la!"
ra: *rah* as in "**ra**men"
Ha: like laughing "ha!"
do: *daw* as in "**daw**n"
mem: *mem* as in "**mem**ory"
Et: *eht* as in "**et**iqu**ette**"

Am-du-si-as Ha-ra-am Ve-ha-bahir

Am: like "I **am**"
du: *doo* as in "**doo**dle"
si: like "see"
as: rhymes with "jazz"
Ha: like laughing "ha!"
ra: *rah* as in "**ra**men"
am: like "I **am**"
Ve: *veh* as in "**ve**t"
ha: like laughing "ha!"
ba: *bah* as in "ba**ba**"
hir: like "hear"

Bu-er Ha-me-na-fetz Ha-sha-ma-yim

Boo: like "Boo!"

er: like "air"
Ha: like laughing "ha!"
me: *meh* as in "**me**t"
na: like "nah"
fetz: *fet* as in "**fet**ter" but ends with *tzuh* sound
Ha: like laughing "ha!"
sha: like "Shah"
ma: *mah* as in "ma**ma**"
yim: *yeem* rhymes with "ream"

Ve-par Shel Ha-se-a-ra Ha-do-mem-et
Am-du-si-as Ha-ra-am Ve-ha-bahir
Bu-er Ha-me-na-fetz Ha-sha-ma-yim

Temporal Disturbance

This curse sounds mild because it is used to make someone unable to keep track of time. The effects are far from mild because your victim will be late, lost, and overwhelmed by circumstances. You're not going to make them forget what year it is, but you will create a persistent state of temporal confusion that disrupts their daily life. It's like setting their internal clock to perpetual chaos, leaving them disoriented and off-balance. It's especially useful when your victim likes to be on time but struggles to live up to their own expectations.

In its most basic form, you can use this to make somebody miss one or more important appointments. Only direct it with this precision if those appointments are something you need them to miss.

Otherwise, it's better to aim for general disruption and let the magick work its creative might. Your victim might show up late to important meetings, forget crucial dates, and struggle to manage their schedule. Their reputation for reliability takes a hit as they become known for their chronic lateness and disorganisation. They'll feel like they only have themselves to blame for their health and finances deteriorating.

Demons to Invoke

Botis: Known for causing confusion and disorientation, Botis can manipulate the target's perception of time, making them lose track of appointments and deadlines.

Vassago: Specialises in discovering what is hidden and knowing the past and future. Vassago can distort the target's sense of time, causing them to become chronically late and forgetful.

Amon: Known for breaking friendships and causing chaos, Amon can induce temporal confusion, leading the target to mismanage their schedule and miss important events.

Words of Power for Temporal Distubance

Bo-tis Ha-a-vud

Bo: *baw* as in "**baw**l"
tis: *tis* as in "no**tice**"
Ha: like laughing "ha!"
a: rhymes with singing "la!"
vud: *vood* as in "**vood**oo"

Va-sa-go A-vur Sha-ot Me-fu-za-rot

Vah: *vah* as in "**va**ledictory"
sah: *sah* as in "**su**n"
goh: like "Go"
A: rhymes with singing "la!"
vur: *vur* as in "**ver**se"
Sha: like "Shah"
ot: *ot* as in "**ot**ter"
Me: *meh* as in "**me**t"
fu: *foo* as in "**foo**d"
za: *zah* as in "huz**zah**!"
rot: like "rot"

A-mon Le-sha-besh Zri-ma

A: rhymes with singing "la!"
mon: starts with *m* and rhymes with "yawn"
Le: *leh* as in "**le**t"
sha: like "Shah"
besh: besh: starts with *b* and rhymes with "mesh"
Zuh: starts with *z* and rhymes with "duh"
ri: *ree* as in "**ree**d"

ma: *mah* as in "ma**ma**"

Bo-tis Ha-a-vud
Va-sa-go A-vur Sha-ot Me-fu-za-rot
A-mon Le-sha-besh Zri-ma

Confusion Curse

The Confusion Curse is a masterpiece of subtlety and chaos, designed to turn a person's mind into a labyrinth of bewilderment. Imagine them waking up each day with thoughts tangled in a web of confusion, every decision an insurmountable challenge. This ritual is your tool to plunge someone into that very state, leaving them disoriented and unable to think clearly or make rational decisions. It can bring complete mental cluttering that leaves the target questioning their every move.

You've probably shared a class with an overconfident student who always aces every test, which would be okay, except they are always belittling others for their struggles. When you've had enough, use this ritual and watch as their sharp mind begins to falter. Their grades plummet, and the confidence they once exuded turns to panic and frustration. They're left stumbling through their academic life, no longer at the top of the class but a confused and struggling student.

Then there's the neighbourhood organiser who prides herself on managing every community event to perfection. She's always in control, orchestrating every detail with precision. If you disagree with the way she does things, or have a totally unrelated gripe, you can use this ritual to make her organisational skills unravel. She forgets key appointments, confuses schedules, and makes glaring mistakes in her planning. The community starts to lose faith in her abilities, and the once-revered leader becomes a figure of disarray and disappointment.

The brilliance of the Confusion Curse is in its relentless erosion of clarity. The effects are gradual at first but devastating, starting with small lapses and growing into full-blown mental fog. It's like watching a once-clear river slowly fill with silt until it becomes an opaque, muddied mess. The chaos in their mind will spill over into every aspect of their life, causing professional setbacks, personal conflicts, and a pervasive sense of frustration and defeat.

Demons to Invoke

Paimon: Paimon's ability to create confusion makes him an excellent choice for this curse. His influence can cause the target to experience mental fog and disorientation, making it difficult for them to focus or recall information accurately.

Naberius: Specialises in creating confusion. Naberius can define where and to what degree confusion should occur, ensuring the target's mental state is effectively compromised.

Alloces: Capable of perceiving the future and binding harmful intentions. Alloces can help ensure the confusion impacts the target's ability to plan and anticipate future events, further complicating their life.

Words of Power for the Confusion Curse

Paimon Sh-veel Ha-bil-bul

Pai: like "pie"
mon: starts with *m* and rhymes with "yawn"
Sh: starts with *sh* as in "**shu**sh" and rhymes with "duh"
Ve: *veh* as in "**vet**"
El: *ehl* as in "**elf**"
Ha: like laughing "ha!"
bil: starts with *b* and rhymes with "peel"
bul: *bool* as in "**Boolean**"

Naberius She-me-val-bel Ha-se-khel

Na: like "nah"
Beh: *beh* as in "**bet**"
ri: *ree* as in "**reed**"
us: *uss* as in "**cuss**"
She: *sheh* as in "**shed**"
me: *meh* as in "**met**"
val: *vahl* as in "**val**edictory"
bel: like "bell"
Ha: like laughing "ha!"
se: *seh* as in "**set**"
khel: *khehl* as in "**kel**p" but starts with a coughed *k*

Alloces Ha-me-sa-bel

Al: rhymes with "gull"
lo: like "law"
ces: *kez* as in "choo**kas**"

Ha: like laughing "ha!"
me: *meh* as in "**me**t"
sah: *sah* as in "**su**n"
bel: like "bell"

Paimon Sh-veel Ha-bil-bul
Naberius She-me-val-bel Ha-se-khel
Alloces Ha-me-sa-bel

Breaking Relationships

Create conflict and mistrust in a relationship to the point that it breaks. Be warned that this curse sows deep-seated jealousy and misunderstandings that lead to the gradual breakdown of relationships.

Imagine the seemingly perfect couple who are always inseparable. As the ritual takes effect, seeds of jealousy are planted. Small misunderstandings turn into heated arguments. Innocent interactions are misinterpreted, and trust begins to erode. The once unshakeable bond between them starts to crack under the weight of suspicion.

Or consider the charismatic individual who seems to attract everyone's affection. Suddenly, their charm becomes a source of conflict. Their partner becomes increasingly insecure, questioning every interaction and doubting their intentions. The constant tension leads to frequent arguments, and the relationship that once thrived on mutual admiration turns into a battlefield of accusations and mistrust.

Only use this when the victims are otherwise well and strong. Ironically, if you attack people when they are weakened or harmed, they may forge a bond of solidarity. Use this when you know they are reasonably well and happy, and you will change everything.

When you use this ritual so that you can pick up the pieces and begin a new relationship with one of the victims, never confess to what you have done. It doesn't cause a problem in terms of magick, but it does cause relationship problems. I've witnessed this need to confess, and I urge you to resist it with great strength.

Demons to invoke

Sitri: Expert in inciting love and lust. Sitri can twist these emotions to create misunderstandings and jealousy, turning affection into a source of conflict.

Zepar: Renowned for influencing love and sexual attraction, Zepar can manipulate feelings to create insecurity and doubt within the relationship.

Leraye: Specialises in causing conflict and revealing hidden emotions. Leraye can amplify minor issues into major arguments, ensuring that misunderstandings escalate into significant problems.

Words of Power for Breaking Relationships

Sitri She-mad-lik

Sit: like "seat"
ri: *ree* as in "**ree**d"
She: *sheh* as in "**she**d"
Mad: like "mud"
lik: like "leek"

Zepar She-me-ga-le Re-gesh

Ze: *zeh* as in "**ze**nith"
par: like "par"
She: *sheh* as in "**she**d"
me: *meh* as in "**me**t"
ga: *ga* as in "ga**ga**"
le: *leh* as in "**le**t"
Re: *reh* as in "**re**d"
gesh: starts with *g* as in "**go**" and rhymes with "mesh"

Leraye She-me-vi Me-ri-va

Le: *leh* as in "**le**t"
ra: *rah* as in "**ra**men"
ye: *yeh* as in "**ye**t"
She: *sheh* as in "**she**d"
me: *meh* as in "**me**t"
vi: *vee* as in "**Ve**nus"
Me: *meh* as in "**me**t"
ri: *ree* as in "**ree**d"
va: *vah* as in "**va**ledictory"

Sitri She-mad-lik
Zepar She-me-ga-le Re-gesh
Leraye She-me-vi Me-ri-va

The Art of Destruction

When you use this magick with serious intent, it should be enough to get you the results you seek and deserve. Do not spend your whole magickal life cursing people. These weapons should be used only when you need them so that your attention can return to bettering yourself and your life.

I do not curse often because I know that this magick works. With age comes some restraint and I have found that laughing off minor crimes and misdemeanours can be easier on everyone. I find it easier to forgive because I have a powerful set of weapons at the ready, and I know I can obtain extreme justice when that's what I need.

If you want to know more about the demons' powers and how they can be used to influence money, thoughts and fortune, my book *Goetia Pathworking* goes over this in detail.

I keep my books expensive on purpose. A cheap or free book will never be used with genuine intent, and I urge you to remember that the actual cost is trivial.

I appreciate you, and if there's anything you like about this book, please feel free to review it on Amazon and share your thoughts. Good reviews keep this kind of publishing alive.

Sincerely,

Corwin Hargrove

More from Corwin Hargrove

Goetia Pathworking
Magickal Results from The 72 Demons

Universal Magick
Enochian Rituals of Darkness and Light

Practical Jinn Magick
Rituals to Unleash the Powers of
The Fire Spirits

The Demons of Deception
Rituals to Hide the Truth, Create Confusion
and Conceal Your Actions

The Magick of Influence
Persuade, Control and Dominate with
The Forces of Darkness

Demons of Wrath
The Dark Fires of Attack Magick

Made in the USA
Las Vegas, NV
21 October 2024